195

The CITY of Dragons

BY

LAURENCE YEP

ILLUSTRATED BY

JEAN AND MOU-SIEN TSENG

SCHOLASTIC
HARDCOVER

SCHOLASTIC INC.

New York

Text copyright © 1995 by Laurence Yep

Illustrations copyright © 1995 by Jean Tseng and Mou-sien Tseng

All rights reserved. Published by Scholastic Inc.

SCHOLASTIC HARDCOVER is a registered trademark of Scholastic Inc.

Library of Congress Cataloging-in-Publication Data

Yep, Laurence.

The city of dragons / by Laurence Yep ; illustrated by Jean

and Mou-sien Tseng.

p.   cm.

Summary: A boy with a face so sad that nobody wants to look at him runs away with a caravan of giants to the city of dragons, where his sorrowful face is finally appreciated.

ISBN 0-590-47865-6

[1. Prejudices—Fiction.   2. Giants—Fiction.   3. Dragons—Fiction.   4. China—Fiction.]

I. Tseng, Jean, ill.   II. Tseng,   Mou-sien, ill.   III. Title.

PZ7.Y44Ci   1995

[E]—dc20   94-31909

CIP

AC

12 11 10 9 8 7 6 5 4 3 2 1   5 6 7 8 9/9 0/0

Printed in Singapore   10

First printing, September 1995

The illustrations in this book are watercolor paintings.

Production supervision by Angela Biola

Designed by Claire B. Counihan

To Joanne — L. Y.

To Phoebe and Claire — J. & M. T.

ONCE THERE WAS A BOY with the saddest face in the world. Even when he was happy, everyone who saw him thought he must be sad, and they became sad, too. So that he would not upset anyone, he wore a big straw hat that covered his face.

When it was almost time for the harvest festival, the village elders politely asked his parents if they wouldn't mind keeping him at home. "We couldn't ask for a nicer or politer boy," the elders explained, "but the hat does not work. He makes everyone uncomfortable because they're afraid the hat will fall off, and they'll wind up crying. And at the harvest festival that would never do."

For the sake of the clan, his parents agreed to keep him at home. As the festival began, they stayed inside listening sadly to the celebrating outside. Finally the boy thought to himself, *It isn't fair to my parents.* So the boy put on his hat and ran away.

He walked on and on until he reached a town where no one
knew him. When he saw a restaurant, he went inside to ask for
work. However, the owner glared at him. "That hat's as big as a
table. If you want a job, you'll have to take it off."

When the boy reluctantly did, the owner chased him out.
"Shoo. People will think my food gave you a bellyache."

Feeling even sadder, the boy put on his hat and wandered on.
I can run away from home, he thought to himself, *but I can't run away
from this face.*

The boy walked on until he wound up on a beach beneath strangely shaped limestone cliffs and could walk no further. He was wondering where to go when the beach rumbled as if in an earthquake.

"Make way. The *fei-le* are coming through," a voice bellowed.

Down the path to the beach came twenty giants, each in a helmet and armor of rhinoceros hide, and with hair so long that it tapped the heels of their boots. Behind each giant was an elephant loaded with baskets and bundles. The chief giant was the tallest and led the caravan. From his helmet hung a long, white scarf.

When he came to the boy, the chief giant halted the caravan. The boy looked up and up and up.

"Please sir," the boy asked, "do you have a job for a hard-working lad?" The boy had to tilt his head way back so the giant could see under his hat.

"What's wrong, boy?" the giant demanded.

The boy quickly lowered his hat. "Nothing."

As the other giants gathered around the boy, the chief giant peered under the boy's hat. "You look like you're going to blubber any moment."

Another giant patted the boy on the hat. "There, there. Go on and have a good cry. Don't try to be brave."

"But I'm not being brave," the boy insisted.

The chief giant gazed at him sympathetically. "You're tougher than elephant hide, aren't you? Something must be dreadfully wrong from the looks of you."

And the more the boy denied it, the braver the giants thought he was until the giants wound up crying themselves.

Wiping at his eyes, the leader declared, "This boy is so brave he puts us all to shame. He has a giant's heart in a boy's body. We could use someone like him."

"A job is a job," the boy replied.

The chief giant swung the boy up on top of his elephant with all the other bundles. "Hold on tight," he warned.

"Where are we going?" the boy asked as the giant splashed unconcernedly into the surf.

"The city of dragons," the chief giant said as a wave crashed over him and he disappeared from sight. Before the boy could quit his new job, his mount plunged under the water.

The giants and elephants looked as if they were crashing through a silvery mirror. From beneath their helmets, the giants' long hair flowed out like wild, black storm clouds.

To his relief, the boy realized that he was still breathing. Through some magic of the giants, they and the boy and their pack elephants could breathe as easily in the ocean as on the land.

Halfway down the slope, the sand gave way to rock where a bed of monstrous clams grew, each large enough to swallow an elephant whole.

"My armor won't fit you," the chief giant told the boy, "but maybe my helmet will give you some protection. Take off your hat."

The chief giant placed his helmet over the boy's head. It was so big that it covered the boy's face.

Then all the giants drew their swords as the caravan picked its way carefully among the giant clams.

On the seafloor, giant crabs with sharp pincers scuttled toward them out of a forest of seaweed. The giants fought them off cheerfully as if they were so many bugs. Beyond the forest, a school of sharks darted in; but the giants shooed them away as if they were pigeons.

Eventually the travelers came to a great plain where a town glowed with a soft, ghostly light. Young dragons swam up to greet the giants and pet the elephants. They circled around the boy inquisitively. "You're the shortest giant we've ever seen."

However, the boy was afraid his face might upset the dragons. So he covered his mouth with the dangling scarf and said nothing.

At the edge of the town, the dragon elder waited with piles of sparkling silk, light as mist. The chief giant looked around. "This is all very fine for the tourist trade; but where are the pearls?"

The dragon elder heaved a heavy sigh. "Alas, we've tried our best to get them, but nothing works."

The chief giant frowned in worry. "We make our profit on the pearls. Without them, we could lose everything."

"If you can do better, you're welcome to try — and a blessing on you if you succeed." The dragon elder led the giants and the boy to a large building.

Inside the high-ceilinged building, dragons drew the fibers of giant shellfish through their claws to make fine thread. Still other dragons wove the thread into silk with loud *click-clacks* on their looms.

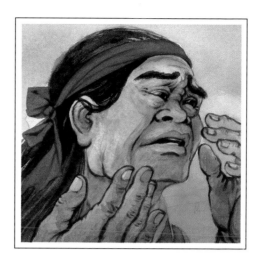

At the rear of the building many scalloped bowls sat all in a row. And behind every bowl sat a dragon; and over the head of each, hovered another dragon, who whispered of disasters, of lost loves, of terrible deaths, of cruel wrongs.

"Those are the saddest stories I've ever heard," the boy declared.

The dragon elder sighed. "The trouble is that they have heard them all. Nothing will make them cry anymore."

The chief giant tried telling a story about a giant who tragically shrank to the size of a flea and could no longer marry his love. But a dragon maiden yawned and politely covered her mouth with a paw. "We've already heard that one."

At that moment, the boy shoved forward and took off his helmet.

The dragon maiden peered curiously at the boy. "You must have some awful tale."

"The worst," the chief giant chimed in. "So awful he won't even talk about it."

"You poor boy," the dragon maiden said and patted the boy on the head. "I'm sure it would make me weep if you would just tell me."

Though she coaxed and wheedled, the boy said that he felt fine; and each time he insisted, the dragon maiden became more and more convinced he was hiding something tragic. Soon her imagination took over, and the dragon hid her face between her paws.

Suddenly something shiny fell — *plink* — into the bowl. Then a second one appeared. Round and pale white and the size of a berry, it fell — *plink* — after the first.

The boy gasped. The dragon was crying pearls instead of tears.

In no time, the weeping dragon had filled the bowl with pearls; and all around them, the other dragons had begun to weep.

When the dragon had filled three more bowls, she thanked the boy. "My, I haven't had a good cry like that in days. It's such a relief. I just wish we could do something for you."

"Never fear, we'll treat this poor boy right." The chief giant lifted the boy high over his head. "I knew you'd bring us good luck."

Back in the boy's hometown, the villagers imagined all sorts of terrible things had happened to the boy. Everyone was sad and ashamed.

One neighbor apologized to the boy's parents. "We should never have chased your poor boy away."

A clan elder reminded the villagers, "Chung Kuei was the smartest man, but the emperor wouldn't employ him because he was so ugly. We should have judged the boy by what he did and not by the way he looked. We were wrong to ask him to stay away from the harvest festival."

The clanspeople were feeling even worse when suddenly they heard a shout from outside the walls. "Hello in the village. Open the gates!"

When the clanspeople climbed up on the walls, they saw the boy in his old hat. But he was sitting on an elephant. They watched speechlessly as the boy, high upon the swaying elephant, strolled through the village to his own house. When he had slid off with his sack of pearls and his bolts of silk, he told the elephant, "Thank you. Now go home to your master, and if he needs me next year, I'll be ready to travel with him."

With a nod, the elephant carefully swung around and left.

That night and for many nights thereafter, everyone feasted. The boy sat in a place of honor in the new silk coat that his mother had sewn for him. And he did not cover his face. And no one asked him to smile. For the clan remembered the story of Chung Kuei and judged the boy by what he had done — and what he had done fascinated them all. They would never tire of hearing about his adventures in the city of dragons.